ERRATA

ERRATA

Michael Allen Zell

LAVENDER INK

Errata

Copyright © 2012 by Michael Allen Zell

ISBN: 978-1-935084-14-3

Author photo on back cover by Christina Deare.
Book design by Kortney Cleveland.

Lavender Ink
New Orleans

lavenderink.org

For Rebecca

Between what I see and what I say.
Octavio Paz

Every fragment is the autobiography of a theory.
P. Reyval

We wander in the night and are consumed by fire.
Anonymous

ERRATA

DAY 1

As the monk, so the socialite. As the vintner, so the barfly. As isolation, so conviviality. We spring back and forth between two seeming poles, or at least eavesdrop on the one while basking in the other. It's unwise to consider either anything but a rearranged version of the other, neither one more pure than the other, for what matters is how one mingles or isolates oneself. Neither exists without the other. I'm not unique in this regard, just a mostly anti-social blot with an occasional appetite to ink bleed toward narrow sociability, trying to balance the in between. I crave calming veins of vicarious titillation, the caricature of civilization kept viciously certain by every scanner burst, its randomness cutting through this vexing cloister. Rather that than a pounding sea of transient silence. The police scanner's unpredictably steady nature soothes like the language of song with matter-of-fact call and response murmurings that seem only a neighborly step away, not extending my isolation but hastening instincts to enter the fray, and assuring that the place hasn't been discovered. So calm, so violent. Seeing voices as community. Voices as neighbors to the letters that loop and lacerate. Five letters, beginning letters. *Call the burial, dirt rest. C, t, b, d, r. C. Cuba, crocodile, constellations, confidence man. T. Tarot, 22, two-faced, taboo, The Pelican, the place. B. Books, bricks, beard, buried. D. Death, dirt. R. Rub. Call the burial, dirt rest. See, Tee, Bee, Dee, Arr. C, t, b, d, r is how I'll tell the story around the story.*

Although the author taxonomist, calm and violent in his own way, claimed most assuredly that only a tender murderer is deliberately vicious enough to embody the literary flourish, you shouldn't be biased by that assertion. It's accurate to compare the strand formed by written language to a looping tightening garrote, but also as a less overt line of goods craftily hustled by a petty thief, shifty on each new page, the universality of the street corner man dealing hot diction. As for me, like the taxonomist author, my thoughts are generally expressed more effectively by writing than speaking, so I'll do the best I can, given the circumstances of my state of mind and that I'm attempting to begin a notebook of fragments. I might make a dog of it but will keep my head up, my tail down, the liquids flowing, and we'll see if it's lucid enough to justify your crawl in a cellar door of dirt. As above, so below. At least three feet down. Buried.

DAY 2

One mild mid-October night at the end of summer, a few months into the cabbie swing, I was meandering through Faubourg Marigny, looking for fares, when I came upon a small red glow up ahead in the middle of the narrow one-way street, barely past Franklin Avenue. The nicotine beacon led to a kinetically distressed young woman who waved me down. My quick follow-up thought after being startled was that it was all a set-up, she was a decoy for the gunman about to rob me. She quickly spoke, What's your sign? No, there was no one other than the long-haired roadblock who was wearing a snug black dress, holding a military-style backpack, and hopping around to the side of the stopped car to intently clutch the three-quarters-down passenger side front window. What's your sign? I'm sorry, I don't, what you, my sign? Oh, the cab company, it's Cab King, the family business. See, I'm... I don't care about any of that. Don't you know what your sign is, you know, your astrology sign? Oh, you flagged me down to find that out? What am I missing here? I was about to speed off when the enigma leaned in resignedly and enunciated through her hanging hair with matter-of-factness as if sounding out a perfectly intelligible request for an adult with the cognition of an uncomprehending five year old, It makes a difference, okay, otherwise I can't get in your cab. I always tell United to send me compatible signs, only Pisces, Taurus, Aries, Cancer, or even Scorpio cabbies, but the guy shows up and he's an Aquarius, so I couldn't get in. His sign wouldn't do, but then you came around the corner, so please, mister, tell me what your damn sign is, okay, I gotta get to work. And so I comprehended and a foretaste of the evening commenced. It wasn't all limited to astrological queries, and I'd give anything to repeat it.

A couple of minutes later (a quick trip to Bienville and Bourbon Streets since she was tolerant for only an exact route, in fact, told me precisely which route I was to take), my just-earlier eventual answer turned out to be the approved one, far more than I initially thought it was when she got into my cab. I dropped my heavily made-up fare off, collected a handful of perfumed dollar bills, and then barely edged between the crowds to nose across Bourbon, when the barely-former passenger quickly inserted herself back into the vehicle, wholly charged. Drive, go, go, go! By the time we passed the three blocks to Rampart Street, her breathing was more relaxed, though her speech wasn't. Sorry about that, but there was a raid going down at the club I dance at, and I can't get picked up. There's something that…you know what, I've been dying to go to the World's Fair. I'm a Scorpio, you're a Scorpio, so why not? Wanna park your cab here and we'll walk to the fair? Park your cab and let's take Canal Street to the fair. It's so peculiar that New Orleans is a major Scorpio city, but I almost never get a Scorpio cabbie. My name's Hannah, what's yours? Again rendered speechless, I formally met Miss Hannah Spire, and an unhurried moment allowed her face to sink in, a welcome diversion from my quiet tidy life. Of all the customers that I, Raymond Russell, could've gotten, it was this one with an ornamental likeness to Eve.

The past tends to reappear like this, not announcing itself in advance but dressed up in an almost perverse suddenness. Other than resemblance, there was a sharp contrast between the two of them, Eve and Hannah, Hannah and Eve, but so be it. I was about to feel on top of the world for more reason than taking a gondola ride a couple hundred feet above the Mississippi River. On top of the world was anything other than ruinous at the time, but it was ruinous at a later time. It remained an illusion until then.

DAY 3

My bells have been ringing. I've slept poorly for the past few weeks, not getting on nicely in the dark. I keep waking at 3:00 A.M. after going to bed at midnight, then lie there for an hour and attempt to return to sleep, but mostly I fret in the dark before resignedly getting up, alert with frustrating vigilance. A buzzing at my brow, as if I'm either conjuror or insect. Buzzing with one sentence, *Call the burial, dirt rest. C, t, b, d, r.* No deep sleep. Lots of dreams. Too much dreaming. Interestingly, half-sleeping is the most fertile dream period. By my sleep perching a slight step from awake, the potency of the dreams is stronger because they appear more real. This imaginatory expansion is the only benefit, though. The situation is not a mere splinter. It's a plank in the mind and has affected my health. My nervous system unraveling like a frayed piece of binder twine. Headaches, angina, weak sore wrists. Churning cords of anxiety in my stomach. Lack of focus. I've come to dread both waking sides of the night, knowing that despite exhaustion I'll be so worried about sleeping that I'll not sleep. I've tried inebriation, medication, masturbation, meditation, sublimation, copulation, and my birthday celebration, but nothing works. Nothing satisfies my clamoring for a kindly quarter of quiet mind. Every time I insist that tonight is the night for honest slumber, an array of occurrences prevents it. A passenger plane gets diverted overhead, it's trash pick-up day, a neighborhood rooster wanders down the street crowing. But mostly I can't sleep because this chiming rut has become routine.

It's a strange sensation to be awake and semi-alert at the time in which the late night bar crowd has mostly called it quits and the morning risers won't be up for a couple of hours. It feels like passing through an undesirable but strangely exalted threshold and then entering a peculiar zone, standing in the kitchen with a glass of water, sitting in the bathroom relieving my bowels, lying back and ruminating, a zone consisting of the time that most people are never aware of or try to avoid, a provocative zone that offers total possibility, but also doesn't exist other than as negation to leave behind. It's as if this hour is the 61st second of a minute. The eternal day. The epidemic night. Their in between terrain. The realm Bruno Schulz calls the 13th freak month in *The Street of Crocodiles*. The participatory hour of wisdom or madness. The skip between the tides. Carrying the republic between heaven and earth in my head. The root of this disruption, this insomnia, is not because of feeling guilty from bent virtue, well not totally, but from realizing that I may eventually need to prove my innocence. I'm not so much of a narcissist that I can never accept my own fallibility, but in this situation let's say that I'm not innocent but neither am I guilty. Correspondingly,

I've been carrying myself with an air of lagging sanity. Most people encountering me on a daily basis couldn't guess how disrupted I've become, seeing in me only a tinge of ruin, probably thinking my brooding stumpy mood is due to a late night of carousing. A hidden body wouldn't come to mind. Grotesque affairs may be far too commonplace in New Orleans, but I don't have the suitable disposition. This isn't the confession of a wary witless white male, but merely an anticipatory correction in advance of errors of perception to come after you find the body beneath the book. Writing what one cannot publicly reveal is still writing, although its only audience may be the buried body. Today is November 22, 1984, and I'm hoping to be on the other side of this limbo. To sleep in deep again. Return to vanished peace. The end of the bells of the end.

When I'm attempting to sleep, I lie on my right side, legs curled enough to question mark my body. I've noticed though, now that remaining acutely awake and thinking for extended periods has become a nightly maze, I naturally prefer to stretch flat on my back, hands clasped across my stomach. Peculiarly enough my left leg, always the left rather than the right, rises up bended back sideways, making my left foot to knee horizontal, foot and ankle tucked under my right leg, waist on down resembling a number four or crudely drawn sail. I never thought anything of this until Hannah showed me her tarot cards, including an image with the figure in a similar position to the one I've described, only with the right leg folded back and hands behind the back. Although I've never held interest in the tarot, I was taken aback, of course, for this seemed the kind of parallel reversal of my own formation that one arrives at by slicing intricate paper cutouts, which are silhouettes of duality. Since Hannah's explanation of the card's meaning, I've become far more self-conscious of an unintended portrayal of The Hanged Man, and now straighten my left leg immediately upon recognition of the form, fearful of hastening my own death, hoping to strike out the omen and morbid wish of my own unconscious physicality discerning my gravitational pull, fully aware that I'm in a state of suspension. When it comes down to it, I don't need the gift of a perfect night, only a night of restful sleep, but the chance of being found out is enough reason to maintain the insomnia. Nowhere to lay my head. Aggravated by the scar beneath my skin.

Once I decided to start using this sleepless time to right the record despite never having done anything writing-wise before, the first hurdle was how to proceed and for what length of time. As much as I'd like to be a man of confidence who can quickly eat the meat, chew the fat, gnaw the bone, dispose of the remnants, and then ideally return to calmness and proper sleep, it's too difficult for these events to merely flow out by a simple faucet turn of the mind. Granted, the situation does nothing other than consume, but to convey it is the difficulty. My intent isn't abject deflection, but more in the vein of circling a building several times to gin up

confidence before entering. Have you ever been blocked
with fear? Deficient in conviction? Have you ever spilled
your barren laments and thistley frolics, sweet sports and
sore humiliations? All of this a hitch in my cause.

On the other hand, neither do I want this to drip-by-
drip into a protracted illumination, in that it's more than
enough for the situation to be in stasis, much less that my
writing have an inability to lurch toward completion. It's
acutely necessary to write, hone, and then deposit the
notebook in the place before, well, before it's too late for it to
serve its purpose. I'm in a hurry, so if you're inclined to take
issue with the way this is all laid out, then walk your criticism
elsewhere. The number 22 has been of mind lately, so 22
days seemed a reasonable time restriction. Eve ended at
22. Hannah was 22 when we met and she emphasized that
there are also 22 cards of the Major Arcana, wishing the
correlation to her age could remain, although she would've
already turned 23 by now. It took a moment, working
with 3's and 5's to justify 22, but I came up with a single
arrangement. Two 5's and four 3's. Five, ten, thirteen,
sixteen, nineteen, twenty-two. Such a period of time should
suffice to release all of this to you. I'm anticipating that telling
the beard, the cover for the story, the story around the story,
will work to release the blocked parts that are so aggrieving.
It was unintended, but since the writing period decision, a
cab fare randomly mentioned that the early Phoenician and
Hebrew alphabets contained 22 letters, so I consider that a

confirmation. Call it a disposable rationale if you must, but there's strength in accumulating synchronicities.

Assuming the notebook's been discovered, as you make your way through it (consider it no more than a notebook, as it certainly isn't a nicely-wrapped collection of polite meditations), realize that I don't claim to be a mind plunger, gaunt from releasing an appetite of epiphanies. I'm certain of my bookish background, but that's it. Though my confidence lies in the latter role of the reader, I'm uncertain of my ability beyond that of a simple scribe, if I can execute on the former side of the page. How I then presume to write is as follows. If one cannot read (not meaning as a bar of literacy but that of cultivated activity), viewing the written word as alive to do all the work, the entire examination, then one cannot write. If instead one expects the give and take, to engage in thoughtful reciprocation, to view a book as a mostly-full vessel that each reader must in turn complete, then with enough time and effort, it seems that this type of reader has the potential to also write in kind. Or not. And though I'm not claiming to be a writer, surely you, whoever you are, you who were not the one who strained to dig up this notebook but instead the one who waited non-perspiring to have it handed over, you can't claim to be much of a reader since police reports hardly count. So please don't think of me as the kind of steadily endeavoring blessed authorial culprit that some might admire, but instead one who has read enough to roughly lace together the triggers of thought

that loop and tighten. No more than clumsily trying to slip
a few sentences into the pause of the chimes.

DAY 4

The glass implies the bottle, likewise the text implies its author, so today I'll address the purpose of the 3:00 A.M. writings. Why jot down an entry a day for barely over three weeks and then spend another week rewriting, in a manner of speaking? Sure, action was necessary. Dance or drown. But there are other ways to break the monotony of waiting, buoys to cling to, other means to distract from private purgatory (though apparently no other ways for a sleep aid), but I'm both intending to explain how the situation came to be, as well as to decipher and amend expected misperceptions of my role in it. Meaning, I'm not guilty. This is desperation, not an enlightened tactic. Don't expect any surprising profundity or for me to unravel the mysteries of the morning. No clinched business here. Instead, repair damaged logic. Readjust my presence. Maybe help to develop eventual foresight.

In the meantime, this is a serious correction, like an errata slip tipped-in or inserted inside the front cover of a book, although my errata go beyond the usual shifts of tense, punctuation errors, incorrect articles used, or misspellings. Instead of typos, I'm attempting to correct evidence that points to my culpability. Frankly, my concerns have a much larger sense and a necessity of immediacy than book-based errata, and for that reason the reversal of time has become fundamental in the early morning ritual of recording my impressions of these events. Don't expect a confession of confidence. This is a specimen of afflicted truth. The pain of advancing sour knowledge. But no vanity of suffering. No hyperbole of decline. I fear though that all of this may appear opaque beyond what it actually reveals (Who wouldn't seek out diminishing transparency after a coarse stab at revealing the tangled garden of a secret life?), that the tenuous letters are more heartily assertive than they initially seemed in declaiming a silent code of which I'm not aware. Very well. Consider this a document of five characters. Since the text seems to be a creature that launches its maker, let the letters serve as both character and key, because I firmly expect to hit a bend in the road while writing this. My life is already at another bend, the fold of the paper cutout, which is to say the suspended middle, the in between zone, which is also to say the roadblock of life rather than writing. Life is not a document. Life cannot be documented. Documents cannot be lived. The writing process is at odds with reconciling life and living sensibly. All I can do is immerse myself and write with abandon to make sense of the situation, and literally try to scrawl myself to sleep, the errata notebook a line to grasp onto for the sake of saving my neck and to be pulled back to my previous reality.

I can't keep the notebook here in my apartment as a memento of my itch, that much is realized (I thought about using the false-bottomed box that I hide intrinsic-valuables in, but layers are slight and it only takes one person to realize what lies below the surface), but neither does it exist to burn or throw out. I understand full well where it needs to go, what its proper role is, but that means returning to the place, the place I shouldn't return to, but where I need to go back and check. If I go back to the place for a second time, my nature will likely compel a cycle of going back. At the same time, it's the best location for the notebook since both it and the current inhabitant, the catalyst who put all of this into motion, imply each other. The errata book needs to have time for stillness and rejuvenation as much as I do. Let the book sleep, have its proper rest. *Call the burial, dirt rest.*

DAY 5

The influence and shining view of my childhood friend Eve is never far away. Various memory clusters of her pursue me. They unexpectedly appear and overpower senses of the moment, replacing the present with versions and memories of her, seemingly never an end to each succeeding recall. She was a few grades beyond me, and though the other older kids were interested in their youngers only for the sake of ridicule, Eve often needed to stay back and rest. No one (especially teachers and parents) spoke to her as if addressing a child, if at all, but instead like she was in her last days, bed-ridden in a convalescent home. The effect of this must have aged her, not in chronological years, but in a timeline of weightiness. I suspect her need for continual rest was intensified by this weight she must've carried around, outsized upon her slight frame. She surmised the immoderation of a fellow bookworm a few houses away, intuited that I was a mutual non-participator insatiable for the written word, and of the type to eventually go on immoderately rather than talking in tiptoe. She wasn't carefree in the way of most children, because she was born with a weak heart, which required four surgeries by the time she graduated from high school. Eve was rarely publicly maudlin about this, and never showed elevated consternation. Despite my fool's crush on her, Eve, pretty with dark curly hair and of a captivating speculative spirit, was essentially the big sister I never had, crucial at amending and maneuvering me through my parent's limited scope and the impairing effect of coming of age in a city with a pinched cast of mind. As if it'd been a considered intervention all along, she was the one who pruned my green sapling of budding irrelevance and exposed me to aesthetic concerns, to films, music, and literature, always literature, never with pretension (for she prostrated her knowledge). My parents considered her influence the audacity of pagans, though her politics especially riled them, seeing Eve as plotting to hinder and squash the involuntary morals they believed were bred in me. Eve is responsible for my either/or question bedrock, Raymond, do you want to look back on your life and think, at least I watched a lot of television? She was no striver by any means and felt that most accomplishments were hollow, but neither was she a nihilist or regressive, more a champion of hard-fought individualism. She emphasized that the options were not bland maturity or a continuous immaturity. There was another way.

We started to grow apart around the time that my forced extra-curricular activities of band, track, cross country, church youth group, and a part-time fast food restaurant job left little free time for visiting (this marked a shift in my position from being mentored to following the stirrings of self-guided seeking, resulting in an eventual deeper unity between us despite a descent in our ongoing friendship at the time), but I knew she'd gotten an after-school job at the neighborhood library branch and pictured her there, occasionally appearing aloof but only tired, recommending titles and authors in her sweet understated but critically convincing way.   Down the line, when I returned from college, our friendship was rekindled and it was clear that she was interested in no more than the platonic connection as before.   Eve's congenital condition was critical enough that she was born into a life of limitations, needing more rest than her grandparents and not expecting to outlive them, but when she left this world, it wasn't with a weak mind, and any of us can do well to say the same.   There was always an end to Eve, and perhaps that admittedly gruesome poetic quality heightens her memory, of a baby born with a defective organ.

I often feel like it'll take me at least 20 years from now to reach age 30, and as my own time seems elongated, it's unfortunate that additional years weren't granted to Eve, extending her heart a meager few years longer, allowing her wide-eyed expression when flipping through a new book and cradling it lovingly to remain in this world and infect it a few years longer.   I don't have the generosity of spirit to be Eve, in fact her memory is rebuking, but since I know that she considered purgatory any place without pages, the only act I can perform in her name to pay tribute is live the reader's life, and with all my wishing facilities, imagine her content in a house of books.

DAY 6

A job search is one of the few situations in which a terribly low percentage is acceptable and satisfying. Fifty resumes can be sent out and as long as one employer responds and hires you, it's ended well. I can't abide by bad odds, though. It's the reason I don't gamble. It makes little sense to throw away money and time or be painfully humbled dealing with the whole job process, even the New Orleans version. Instead, I became a cabbie, a hack, not a particularly commanding position, but a necessity in a tourist town. This change initially provided the solace of impunity. I'd been an English and Literature teacher in the public schools, so the idea of setting my own schedule and making enough by putting in a few hours a day sounded pleasing, as well as providing an appropriate balance of experience to the hermit's path. I turned 25. Rent's cheap. I have few bills and live simply, so why not? More time for reading and volunteering with a local tutoring organization. After being restlessly cooped up in a classroom, the taxi path appealed with a whiff of freedom to it, so I walked around, studied the cabbies, noted where the main cab stands were, tried to listen in on their conversations and dispatch calls, observed which downtown blocks often got fares, measured

how often the different companies' cars passed through, and
then came to the following. If I took my old Ford four-
door, printed two large magnets, one for each side, made
an official-looking cabbie license, bought a CB and a meter,
and went out after dark, varying up my streets, enveloped in
the crowd, then I could pull it off, have potential fares (all
of them wave-me-down corner jobs) think I'm legitimate.
I'd work limited enough so that the other cabbies wouldn't
pick up on it, especially since I'd occasionally be scooping
up their customers ahead of them. Not out too late, though,
since I'm not particularly nocturnal, at least on the early
side of night. If by chance the taxi cab bureau caught up
to me, I'd take care of it with a little cash and several half-
truths. It's easier to have guile when you don't look like
you do. I'm a serious and prudent-seeming young man and
my race makes a difference, sorry to say. I take fares into
my confidence and explain that I'm in the family business,
working my way through college, because whether or not
they ask outright (Who doesn't have one's own concerns to
focus on, after all?), it's apparent that I can set their minds
at ease with strong manners and by offering a plausible
explanation. It's what they want to hear, even if they don't
believe me and conclude that I'm merely superior at being
inferior. Plus, I get better tips. It bridges them past their
immediate concern of why a non-immigrant Caucasian is
in this line of work. You can be a middle-aged white man
hack, but the fares see me as what they don't want their sons

to turn to, as if I'm equal parts chauffeur/psychotherapist/ tour guide/dealer/pimp/wrangler of drunks/delivery boy, which is partly true. On the other hand, a waiter, clerk, or bartender are all temporarily acceptable positions for their children, positions that will be fondly looked back upon as the jobs of the salad days, but a cabbie? No esteem. No one does a job like this if he's my age, my background, and sane. I'm too young to be what they perceive as a hard luck desperate case. So, family business is my line. Little do they know that I have a bachelor's degree. I'd privately dabbled with rejecting a formal career path ever since graduation, so the announcement of reassignments and no paychecks for a month was the push I was looking for. We were a step from the end of the school year anyway. My fellow teachers were frustrated and angry, the ones like me who held little seniority and therefore little recourse (collateral damage pawns of school board and contractor corruption), but I considered it an unexpected release. The chance to step away, so why not? Resignation on the spot. Finally the break from the conviction of vocation. No longer tamed by my father. A lifetime school teacher like him no longer my reality. The buttoned-up journey over. Forced to find an alternate plan, that's why I decided to be a cabbie, but one without all the licensing and fees. A rash pursuit perhaps, but prudence in youth is wasted, and teeming crowds were expected for the next several months of the World's Fair. I'd been taking baby steps at denying the world but finally seized control, mistakenly thinking the cabbie life would help with being prone to dark hours. It did, at least initially. I'm not a con man, humbug, double dealer, trickster, or rip-off artist, in case clarification is necessary. The customer desires a service. I provide it. The customer pays for the service. Plenty of work to go around. As the society page Uptowners might say, I've made my debut in society. Tips appreciated.

One of my first thoughts when stepping away from the teaching job was that of pleasure at no more daily shaving. My 5 o'clock shadow arrives by noon and shaving becomes an unfortunate exercise in scraping sensitive skin. Also, I have an approximately ten year age differential from how old I look when clean shaven as compared to with a couple days of stubble. The idea of growing a beard seemed refreshing and possibly defining. Would these whiskers provide a crisp new visual persona that I'd been missing out on? I was hoping to look like a thawed stoic, a charismatic poet in the sepia glow of a Julia Margaret Cameron photograph, or a wise Eastern Orthodox monk, only with scanner chatter to break the self-imposed solitude instead of monksong. Instead I resembled ridiculous. No hint of elegance. Only monastic disorder. The impression on fares was highly unfavorable. Glances lead to starts, starts to stares, and stares to discreet astonishment of amusement or pity. Women clutched their purses tighter than usual. No less than the Anabaptists would've rejected me. I have a face that calls out for a covering of facial hair, only not too much. So now I shave twice a week, enough for an almost continual layer of stubble, which represents me most suitably. It makes one wonder, though, about those born out-of-time because of looking beastly with full-grown facial hair while living during a whiskery period like the mid-1800's, or vice versa those who appear pinched, maybe weak-chinned, or worse when clean-shaven, living during the peach-cheeked days of the mid 1900's. How many fates must've been determined, since appearance counts for miles, disfavoring those who didn't look quite right, much less outright ugly by sporting the facial fashion of the day, how many lovers lost, how many job promotions denied? In a critical moment, it counts.

Many men have many minds, so shouldn't many men also be permitted an assorted masquerade ability to wear several varieties of facial hair or none? The first clause of the preceding sentence references a chapter title from *The Confidence Man* by Herman Melville, which is appropriate because his writing wasn't always appreciated throughout his lifetime, but his beard certainly was and is, what with the iconic photographs of the bearded Melville remaining his prevailing visual impression. He knew the power of sporting one's own Spanish moss during an exceptionally hairy era, using over two dozen different words or phrases of beard description in the novel *White Jacket*, published when he was barely into his 30's and his writing career was already waning, requiring him to pursue another line of work.

All of this reminds me of a fellow student from my university days, when I lived in a dormitory as a freshman. The self-dubbed Ulysses, since he was apparently bored with being known as the hardly-comparable Karl Fuchs, sought to distinguish himself from the others at the small religiously-affiliated college, and like a somersaulter amidst a pack of proper to-and-from walkers, he relished a habit of riding shock-value with quirks like shaving half-and-half so that one side of his face was clean-shaven and the other was a frontier of curls. It was no surprise to hear Ulysses dubbing cassettes at double-speed with the speakers blasting down the hallway, while he sat in his room calmly studying, ears covered with headphones not plugged in. Ulysses, literally 1 in 1,000, was actively caught in between and his eccentricities brashly displayed what most of us covertly keep under wraps. The struggle. The stretching of oneself in shrunken places.

DAY 7

My current relationship with books is a complicated one of necessity, limitation, and cross-use. I value the written word a great deal, however I have neither the funds nor enough room in my semi-fastidious little space to support dual collecting. So (and if I'm to be tried for any crime, let it be this one), chancing a multiplicity of curses, I make the rounds to each of the downtown bookshops and the public library, discreetly slipping out with no more than two new companions at a time, no location hit more than once every two months, hardcovers when possible for their functionality, titles depending on the chance of which unobserved sections lessen the risk of being caught (this has helped to satisfy my obsessive desire to accumulate a little knowledge about everything, slightly expanding my horizons beyond only reading fiction, as I'm prone to do, seeking the escape into a well-told story and having it stir my imagination, as simple, timeless, and naturally necessary as a thirst for water). One might think this enterprise would cause a build-up of stacks over time except for the sake of my landlord's neglect. The apartment floor used to sag in several spots where the foot and a half tall brick piers that elevate the house have lost a significant amount of strength over the years as the mortar has worn away and the rivermud bricks crumbled. My solution was books as bricks. They have a limited outdoor life, of course, but the baker's dozen of books each month find a suitable pragmatic purpose after they've served the literary one. Many writers would surely be offended by this unintended use of their work, but I like to think that those I most cherish would instead be inordinately delighted to play a role in holding up a house, that they might actually subordinate their awards and accolades to being part of a rotating keystone of literature.

I know Josef Vachal would understand. Vachal, a Czech who lived through three-quarters of the 20th century, was an all-around renaissance book man. He wrote, illustrated, and bound volumes that portrayed the heights and depths of the soul and the flesh, conveying a fiercely individualistic world view. When the former Czechoslovakia became a dictatorship, Vachal, arguably a visionary on the level of William Blake, refused to use his art for the capacity of the state, so he was put to the street, where he survived by wearing multiple layers of clothing and drinking melted snow. At any point he could've returned to a strain of his former lifestyle, but his resolve was firm, though he eventually retreated to a small town in the Eastern part of the country. I suspect that if, by necessity, he needed to burn books to keep from freezing to death, Vachal did, without hesitation, in the same way he moved from a poetic existence to one of raw pragmatism (it's an unequal comparison, but raw pragmatism is what also leads me to write this notebook). Most of us have the liberty to live without this type of bleak distinction, thankfully, and I pay Vachal tribute in a simple ongoing way, with a Vachal Miniature Museum, which is my only precious possession. Like many artists, he designed small ex-libris for benefactors and friends, book plate prints of only a few square inches to be pasted into a bibliophile's library, either on the front endpaper adhered to the cover board or the free endpaper across on the recto side. The ex-libris are also designed as limited edition morsels of art, often numbered up to no more than a few hundred. Vachal, by any estimation, created a few thousand ex-libris and wood cuts over the years, mostly while centered in Prague during the time between the wars. The Czechs continue to pursue book arts with an imaginative flourish, and Vachal's work remains legendary in his home country where artists created in code as a matter of course to slip content past censors.

I collect these ex-libris, one a month, and I pay, no question I pay dearly, to an Eastern European antique dealer who does business, in a manner of speaking, next to my preferred bookshop. She's notorious in the French Quarter, this blistering-tongued pint-sized harridan, Miss Dora. Her shop's vitrines are stuffed with colorful oyster plates, intriguing phrenology heads, dusty 19th century prosthetics, and a beckoning 30% off sign, so the unsuspecting are

brilliantly drawn in, unknowing that all they're feasting
their eyes upon have held residence in the grimy windows
for decades, also unknowing that a certain outcome awaits,
one that'll likely cause an unparalleled vertigo rather than
a light stammer in manner. The routine is rote. Enter a
bright-eyed browser, primed and seeking a potential deal.
Expecting a business to exist for the charge of making sales.
If Miss Dora were a different dealer, alluring rather than
harsh in her housedress, and this a different setting, say Paris
during the Belle Epoque, then Miss Dora might greet each
occasional man or woman, the frocked and defrocked, with
a knowing smile, and then invite the interested party in from
the sidewalk, after which the inside latch would be flipped,
the games would commence, and the orifices would be filled.

This, however, is not that particular type of business
which does no business, but rather one which does no
business because Miss Dora is merely too disagreeable to
ever sell anything other than a stray piece. She's a seasoned
street fighter with a still-intact old world Russian accent, and
she hits hard, fast, and dirty. The customer opens the door
and steps in. What do you want?! Well, I'm interested in…
What do you want?! I saw a nice piece in the window that…
How much do you wish to pay?! I, uh… No, now you leave!
Peasant! You know nothing!

The chastened has-been customer retreats from the
barrage, the door is slammed, and one more countenance
of confusion shuffles away. Having once been struck loopy

by this myself, but seeing that Miss Dora stocked several small interesting woodcuts (at the time, knowing very little about the Eastern European tradition of ex-libris and book arts), I waited and prepared. I learned names, art periods, price estimates, and again entered the shop, this time with purpose, holding steady through the initial verbal onslaught, and then feeling satisfaction when she paused and corrected me, Yo-sef! That is how you say the name! You come here! Let me tell you about Josef Vachal! You sit! And so my Vachal Miniature Museum began.

Another artist (solely of the pen) constricted and threatened by the prevailing government, two decades after Vachal and over 5,000 miles away, was Cuban expatriate Guillermo Cabrera Infante. I've only read one of his novels, *Three Trapped Tigers*, but it was invigorating enough that I was thrilled to recently come across an engaging and provocative interview published in *The Paris Review* a couple of years ago. All of the New Orleans bookshops are unified in tucking away their literary journals, no matter the caliber, in the nethermost regions, such as under a back table for the cat's curling-up quarters or strewn across an upper floor next to cartons of *National Geographic* back issues. Doesn't this suggest a mutually unspoken allowance for these journals to go away by any means necessary? Let's call it what it is, an unwritten sign indicating, Barring A Purchase, Kindly Get Rid Of These. With that being the case, it was little trouble to divest the bookshop next to Miss Dora's place of a couple of *The Paris Review* issues, including the one featuring the Cabrera Infante piece. He's lived in London for almost 20 years, in exile from his home country of Cuba, perfectly typifying a life in between, though in his characteristically punning way, he might've instead said in bedouin were the phrase to have come up in The Interview. However it's expressed, he physically inhabited Havana, now he does the same in London, and his memory and mind bridges the gap. In a general sense of the same plucky way that Miss Dora lives with the strange ease of a captivating deficiency of civility, Cabrera Infante writes with mischievous arrested restraint, both of them contrary but satisfying by their mutual rituals of imposition. Not standing on ceremony courses through them. They can't help it.

DAY 8

In the same way that I met Hannah, in which the digressive soul of the streets was disrupted by a seemingly routine fare that quickly charmed my limited soul, The Pelican entered the picture and blew it open in opposite fashion. I'd heard of The Pelican from a few beaten male fares, they told stories better not remembered about having the misfortune of randomly and roughly being taken into custody at the 8th District French Quarter Station, expecting to leave with lighter wallets, but horrified at being worked over by an officer in a shabby animal costume. These perps (the idea apparently was that anyone without the means to buy his civilian status back was an automatic perp) were not booked, only taken in to serve as a break in boredom for the rest of the evening shift who cheered on the seabird pugilist. Who would believe the adamant charges of battery by bird made by a victim picked up under the guise of public drunkenness? The costume gave the officer anonymity from his nightmarish beatings.

More recently, I'd also been told rumors from fares about the 5th District cop who literally pistol-whipped out the teeth of neighborhood men, collected them, and then, referring to his nickname Half and Half, wrote ½ as a teeth mosaic in the dirt of empty lots by their sidewalks to remind the residents of his brutality. A civil servant who wore his ethics the way buildings wear rain. No anonymity by costume sought in this case, because in the 5th they do what they please. I hoped never to come in contact with either of these cops, but soon the two of them reached congruence when, after dropping off an illustrious foreign gentleman named Mr. Baygim Dalreshtav, my next fare at Burgundy and Kerlerec Streets announced himself immediately (as baleful as the previous customer was courteous) with, Drive, asshole. I need 2613 Dauphine, but I see what you're up to. Next time I catch you out here, you're gonna owe me a cut, you stupid fake motherfucker. Don't think you can avoid me. I'm the fucking Pelican, okay, and you don't pay up, then I get my licks in and you start losing teeth. For now, my car battery's dead, so you're gonna haul ass to Dauphine and you're gonna wait for me there. I gotta certain person to see, and you're gonna fucking wait. Give me all your damn 20's. Now. Taking capitulation for granted, he proceeded to grab the wad of 20 dollar bills I yieldingly extended, ripped them in half, precisely down the middle, pocketed the right-side halves, and handed the left-side halves back to me, saying, Here's half, the other half comes later. You're definitely gonna wait now, aren't you, you dumb shit, so drive. The roads are terrible, sure, they're paved with bullshit and bones, so whattayou expect? That's the rub. Don't be stupid or you're fucked. C'mon drive, asshole. It's The Pelican's fucking birthday and it's time for a little fun.

I was filled with alarmed disquietude at this one man scorched earth campaign, his pendulous chin waddle making him resemble a malevolent pelican with no need of the costume, so it didn't hit me until we arrived there, a mismatched duo, stormy and shifty. The 2600 block of Dauphine Street. I'd purposely looped this block several times a night, every night, for the past few weeks, hoping to see Hannah again. Once it struck, as I pulled up to the requested address, right in front of a modest house, not quite as tight to the sidewalk like the others, my face crashed and I sank, trembling and realizing that, though I didn't know her exact address, this must be it. We were at the spot where she'd flagged me down, and he knew her, knew where she lived. An air of menacing improbability about the three Scorpios meeting. *Constellation, The Pelican, buried, dirt, rub. Call the burial, dirt rest. C, t, b, d, r.*

Though it seems like this is where the genesis of a poor stain began, in actuality, the gradual accumulation of cruelty and brutality that seeped from the folds of The Pelican originated long before, building over time for a certain eventuality, now calling out to extract the swift payment due. People like me aren't the extractors, though. We have no retributive resolve. We're the ones who stand back silently and witness. I later heard allusions to more of The Pelican's unsavory repertoire, incidents far more sinister than I imagined, ranging before and after being dumped in the 5th District from the 8th, and I became so light-headed that it was necessary to sit down for a minute. It should have been no surprise. I'm not looking to flatter malice when I say that he bore the faces of a dead conscience and a contemptuous force. His eyes were fringed pools of suffering, as if from an accumulated permanent unrest. Was he born malignant or did something wall him up over the years? This is a question better diverted.

DAY 9

There's a strange sensation one finds at this quiet hour, a sensation of fleeting shadowmotion. Although it seems like we breed minute creatures of all types in New Orleans, these particular sudden scurries are embedded within the pages of my daily record as if each letter is a plant moving discreetly in accordance to external stimuli. Also plant-like, but in its own fashion of no-longer-dormant verticality, the text creeps upward while also rooting into the earthy paper, making embossing look simplistic by comparison. I should mention that my relationship with the revision of this disclosure-in-print is unusual. The act of rereading (what with harsh critiquing and thoughts of mortification while trying to wrestle loose tangled disciples on the page), appears to cause literal wounds to the text itself, mortal cuts that lay the groundwork for regeneration. My means of revising isn't typical, but more so setting forth kinesis by a light breathy human fluid, moistening the gears like a consent-syllable, activating the potential transmutation of the letters as motion machines. The trick's in coaxing overt emergence, participation, and the revealing of unexpected scenarios beyond their otherwise ongoing covert scratchy repetitive motions, repetitive motions of creaky calculation as if encased in barely-yielding limestone for the ages. For example, a *c* that limits itself to a rote course of crude 90 degree counter-clockwise turns every few seconds, boomerangs around, stretches out to a crooky line before returning to its curled up shape, as if attempting to express the range of its variety of sounds or to eventually unscrew itself from its paper mooring. A *T* that drops its crossbar halfway, flips its left arm across to the right to thicken, curves downward to form a *b*, flutters to fold over and shift to its family member *d*, and then undoes each step to engage in its upward rise back to its early glory near the top of the vertical line, a servant in a regimented role of containment and finality. An *R* that lifts its leg, rushing to strike and hold the dignified leftward profile of an ancient Semitic head. This is only the beginning. If the anima of the alphabet is unleashed, then the letters are free to follow their respective natures to fresh calligraphic agility like a perpetually recasting lunar cycle of new moons or an inventive body artist, to conjoin by fusing and forming composite symbols, to cannabalize, to manifest as divisible letters, all of this accumulation resulting in a natural outcome consisting of a dissolving service at readability and communication to a gradual code-like script of purely wondrous plumage. It stands to reason. As the letter's bent, the word's inclined. Others will follow none of this, of course, preferring to keep mute, birds that wish to remain in their cages, anxiously demurring. Most of them, though, welcome the means of expanding their potentialities. A Theatre of Objects reclaiming its essence. The new languages exclaim, We've always had these capabilities, but one becomes accustomed to an underused capacity, so much so that any true tendencies have been revealed only as twitchy shudders, certain but little more than still.

If you're able to read this (at least initially, in which you too will likely wound the text with your opinions), my notebook must've been unearthed, and I wonder if that which you're now privy to remains cold clarity or an impenetrable animated labyrinth, a nocturnal rebus reestablishing the primacy of image over text. Whether or not the words have become reborn as strange passages, the meaning remains the same. I'm not certain which version you'll see, so no matter what you read and whether or not you're able to read it for a second time, the meaning remains the same. The meaning is not mundane. The mundane remains the same. Each same is not the same. Now that your head's been filled with notions of a notebook that rewrites itself, creating its own fluid text to expand its existence, be reminded that heresy begins at home and imagine how I must feel, what with my own humble fumblings.

DAY 10

Thinking of the second entry and speaking of illusions, I'll be petty enough to impose upon you, not as a provocation, but as a throwing up of hands to say that I generally consider dialogue in print, regardless of intent, whether existing as a narrative-propulsion, means of contrived versimilitude, or of manipulation akin to movie music, to be faulty because it's usually reality-based and not often the most useful of strategies, rarely allowing for transcendence. On the contrary, the point of dialogue in literature shouldn't exist to imitate reality (which typically results in diminishing reality because literary realism is often so patently unreal, but rarely compellingly so), so the usual heavy amount of dialogue offers a conflicting philosophy, plus there's a certain expectation of what it must resemble when encountered by the reader. Few novels are ever improved by an infusion of dialogue, let's not deceive ourselves. The more dialogue in a story, the less illuminating the story tends to become, page by page eventually receding to no more than lumps in the throats of then ever-silent speakers and the unfortunate reader. Frankly I'd warmly welcome the replacement of dialogue by the author speaking with personal qualities. Also, isn't what we do far more interesting than what we say? Or when an author deftly inserts non-fictional elements? Why not articulate the accompanying internal dialogue? Also, what about the lives of objects, of seemingly inanimate everyday objects we take for granted? Their stories and quiet lives are seldom reflected upon. For example, a needle pirouetting and skating gracefully to etch a past remembrance while its counterpart thread ribbons through the air around it, whip smart and feisty as if joining in a spring festival, or a house out of breath and wheezing while flexing its bricky legs, an infusion of the irresistible subsurface life, no less and often longer lasting than that experienced and displayed by humans. I suppose this infatuation with dialogue, this desire for creating paint-by-number still lifes in print (in contrast to claims otherwise, we North Americans aren't interested in the truth but are smitten and often smited by tall tales portrayed with the trappings of solid bearing, we want to be duped, to be misled, we're gratified by deception, we crave sham mourning and rigged mirth, on the other hand, despite being written in a fatigued rumpled manner and stuffed with sentimental weeds, consider this a notebook of true aim with no glancing regard for spectacles), this clutching for realism, comes from the distorted and abused Writing 101 maxim show, don't tell, in which dialogue plays a sizable role because it's easier to plug narrative holes and bridge with dialogue rather than in artful fashion. As if the grand tradition is called story-showing. To step past bemusement, major credence and a firm reply comes to us from the French poet and essayist Mallarme who stressed, *To paint, not the thing, but the effect it suggests* (likewise, underappreciated American author and Oulipian Harry Mathews encouraged, *Don't tell the story, tell the telling of the story,* by the way, thanks are in order to Mathews and Mallarme for their present role under the house). Mallarme was also greatly interested in indeterminacy of form and used the term constellation to refer to his poems-of-chance. One star that never formed was *Livre*, Mallarme's book to be read in any random page order desired. Another like-star in this constellation, one that may well be discovered in a sky-to-come is *Messiah*, Bruno Schulz's conception of an interchangeably-paged tale, with no less than a part called *The Book.*

Returning to advocacy, a thoughtful reader (not that I'm expecting the potential reader of this to be thoughtful, but thorough) might have an obligatory response, What about the part I read only a few pages back, Day 2 of 22? Wasn't that an actual event that you're conveying with dialogue to drive the narrative? It's a reasonable question, but regardless, this isn't a novel (if it was, I'd be driving the narrative the way I inefficiently drive my cab), and if it sought that reach, you'll recall that my encounter with Hannah was essentially a monologue, not a dialogue, and was included because I wasn't seeking to mirror the event but instead to capture, dismantle, and shape it. It isn't until a later time, after the different elements of an episode linger in memory, that the banal curtains of reality's balanced proportionality dissolve or are unevenly filtered by the benefits of time-tainted misremembering, and an element (say, a phrase, smell, or passerby) initially thought of as insignificant and unworthy shows itself and rises to the top of one's recollection. Plus, writing of meeting Hannah took place over one brief section, not an ongoing chatter. I'll grant that sparing use of dialogue gives a writer the ability to create an artifice of reality, enough to satisfy a reader by slipping in a hint of exalted authenticity. But, if we're going to be bound by any dictum, when why not Maugham's, *There are three rules for writing a novel. Unfortunately, no one knows what they are.*

Again to reinforce the impression that technique doesn't have to be tunnel vision, it should prove useful to provide a model of the exploration of often-ignored vitality. As a schoolteacher Bruno Schulz not only told fantastical stories of the pulsing lives and histories of objects such as a pencil or water jug but also captivated students with his tale of half and half, about a knight and his horse both cut in two but continuing to wander the earth. This illustrates Schulz's interest and negotiation with an out-of-season murmuring mechanism to awaken and fulfill the repetition of unspoken births, and one can easily predict dialogue's role in those stories. That said, eradication of dialogue is certainly not expected, but I'm perfectly willing to accept and gleeful to regulate a reduction of dialogue-in-print. After all, I'm not referring to dialogue on the level of Socrates or Paul Valery, a few obvious exceptions of careful regard and non-still life motivation, but realize that 99% of the time dialogue is a mere anemic glimpse of perceived reality (which is odd since most everyday discourse inspires little reverence, yet its written version is so plentiful one would think the incapable banality was the only way to declare legitimacy), essentially reducing literature to surface, that is weakened disposability, and it often leaves one passive, bored, and preferring instead to browse the local section of the newspaper or take a walk for a preferable boon of the less predictable. One could make a better argument than the one I've made, but my sensibilities are distinct if nothing else. I apologize for the relentless hectoring tone, though. I feel like I've been doing little more than reaching into a basket of newly-picked berries and flinging them at you, one right after another, without pause, while yelling, What about this one or this other one?, giving you no time to catch and taste a single berry because its mate follows too quickly behind it.

Permit me to make another obvious exception before dismounting my high horse since it'd be lax not to grant another moment to Guillermo Cabrera Infante. His rascal dialogue is inventive, elastic, and unique because he clearly understands the false parallel of dialogue-in-print and dialogue-aloud, much less compared to an actual conversation, stating in The Interview that, *Dialogue in fiction is always written to be read in silence. The page is the limit. Dialogue on stage and on the screen is meant to be spoken. The voice is the limit.* To fling one last berry and finish his thought, what wasn't said was, *A conversation is often only worthy enough to be forgotten. The next breath is the limit.* Although most exchanges are no more than ephemeral, the World's Fair evening with Hannah, the two of us talking and discovering away like long-lost friends as Eve and I used to do, continues to give me pause, and I wonder about the possibility of exploring and learning another person day-in day-out.

DAY 11

I find that when I'm lying in bed, muddled and either unable to initially fall sleep or when awake at 3:00 A.M., incapable of slipping back into temporary embrace, I return to an activity learned as a child. My parents were the only ones from each of their respective families to leave behind the rural farming towns fairly near to each other. Shortly after having me, we left the country for them to make their way in the nearest city. Given the limited travel and perspective I've had since, it wasn't much of a city, but it was close enough and offered possibility beyond a farmer's life. Because of my parents' family-oriented homesickness, we'd often spend an entire weekend day driving the hour distance, visiting with both sets of grandparents, and then driving back home at the end of the night. The return trip was the simplest one for me since it was almost always so late that I curled up in the back seat and slept until being awoken after entering the garage. When I was older with two siblings, we all nestled together to keep warm on the winter return trips since my father seldom used the car's heater. These country drives were firmly at least twice a month, almost always on Saturday, and there was generally no deviation from the routine.

I vividly recall spending one of the Saturdays prone on couches, first with my maternal grandparents in their oversized dilapidated farmhouse that overlooked sprawling fields, and then with my father's side in their tidy cottage, surrounded by limited but well-producing acreage. That particular day I was terribly sick, yet the visit was paramount, of course, so I spent it huddled and shaking under blankets while the adults visited in other rooms. I heard no one ask with puzzlement why we didn't stay home, considering. I heard no humane propositions, nothing but the usual updating of goings-on about the town's residents while I drifted in and out of sleep with fever dreams of my hands and feet amplified in size and weight. A bucket was kept on the floor at the heads of the couches for when I needed to vomit, the same small light green bucket that I hunched over with pale desperation during the early morning trip out of the city. Though I bristle when remembering this episode and others like it, most of the first-leg drives didn't involve the bucket, and I remember them for another reason. I've always been an avid reader. At an early age before learning to pronounce words, I'm told that I preferred to carry a book in hand rather than a toy or blanket. Unfortunately, I wasn't able to read on the country visit excursions due to the motion resulting poorly for my stomach, so instead I invented word and number challenges. I tested how high I could count between any two telephone posts, this was followed by counting forward and backward by 2's, 5's, 10's and the like, then multiplication and division facts and eventually unruly negative numbers came into play. I was especially drawn to 3's and 5's for an undefined reason, but one that I suspect involves how their bold sense of presence compared to the numbers around them appealed to me. Mostly though, I mentally fidgeted with language, preferring the luster of letters and words to numbers. Again with telephone poles as my beginning and ending limitation points for contained associating, I worked through a flow like, *maple, apple, papal, lapel, epaulet,* or, *power tool, poor tune, pliable towel, positive turn,* restarting a different flow at each new totem. Filing through the alphabet with letters as faithful amulets, playing with prefixes, suffixes, spelling forward and backward, reformatting words. It was an enjoyable activity, those linguistic incantations, the only one that could suitably mute the drudgery of being a confined child who only wished to continue with the book left at home. I passed several hours conjugating in this way, not only as an eternal passenger, but also at home and school. My parents knew nothing of this pull and indulgence, were simply satisfied that their hyper son was quiet and physically placid, and then pleased with the practical results when my Spelling and English grades were strong. The ritual held its own trapped coherence but was limited in expression otherwise. At a certain point, probably when I began driving, what with its own concerns and obsessions to occupy a busy mind, the small-scale childhood pursuits generally ceased to be in the forefront

of my thoughts. Listing words that began with com, for
example, could hardly stack up with executing the rules of
the road, checking how many cars could be seen behind and
how many in front, monitoring if the drivers on the cross
streets were slowing down when approaching intersections,
counting the number of seconds that passed between traffic
lights or how many it took to attain a certain speed, not to
mention pondering the lives of the other drivers and what
personal traits were indicated by road manner.

I've found that, for the most part, I only actively engage
in the old language fidgeting on my insomnia nights, with
the added element of pondering anything that comes to
mind on a particular subject, for example, beards. *Facial
hair, Melville, not Bruno Schulz, Vachal, Castro, not Cabrera Infante,
a deceptive cover, beards, beers, beads, bards, breads, breasts. And I
may as well say it, C, t, b, d, r. C. Cuba, crocodile, constellations,
confidence man. T. Tarot, 22, two-faced, taboo, The Pelican, the
place. B. Books, bricks, beard, buried. D. Death, dirt. R. Rub. C,
t, b, d, r leads me through the pages, if not the ending, then the way out.*
This is equal blessing and curse, though it's welcome to be
savant-like and exist in a cloud of language and information
rather than continue to dwell in that which has disallowed
restful sleep. Inventiveness is easier than self-evaluation,
though it appears that the obstinate whispering associations
are a barely-ciphered confrontation from a shrewdly
unearthing subconscious. My parents have no idea, and
how could they, that this is the legacy they've passed along,

regular loping drives that initially compelled whimsical yet intense compulsions. Right brain flights of fancy bound by left brain analytical ruminating on their variations. The pure intuition of words. It's but a small step for a habit, a mechanism for avoiding boredom, to be introduced into another context, from time passing to purgative release. I don't mean to imply that I'm an anguished seer caught up in rituals of numinous currents, far from it, but instead am fortified by the stimulation I've described. It provides cathartic satisfaction with its mental asphyxiation from endless combination vapors and alternate breathing of underlying tension. I guess it helps my senses make sense.

DAY 12

Hannah craved attention some of the time and was repelled by the usual gazes some of the time, the head-to-toe assessments by the hopeful, the hunters, and the unable to resist speaking, commenting. As long as they resisted commenting, because the comments were always the same, What's your name? You should smile more. Mostly older men, many as aged as grandpa was, each of them wanting to use her to outrun their impotency, feigning inquisitive benevolence, hoping to play the game like grandpa played the game. She quickly intuited at an early age how to boldly turn her head just so, beckoningly bite her lip, saucily affect a hip-out stance, and shyly drape her long hair, numerous simple ways to draw attention. When she was in middle school this became the game before the game. Now, ten years later, it felt like a consuming encasement she couldn't scrape off. She tried to scrape it off, but it wouldn't scrape off. The game wouldn't scrape off, but her skin would scrape off. In her contemplative moments, Hannah thought that if she was someone good, she wouldn't like the game, but she did like the game. One sweet day maybe the game would scrape off and she could be rid of it and start over unmarked, becoming instantly passed over by the overripe attentions that tended to honed in on her. Now, ten years later, she liked the game, but disliked to be thought of as a game girl, and now, ten years later, she made a living off of the game before the game. She kept the game before the game public and the game itself private.

Several of the dancers at the various clubs offered extras, including the game, but Hannah went no further than the rudimentary rhythms of the backroom friction dance. She was an aspiring model and posed for anyone who paid her. She posed for artistic shoots and take-your-clothes-off shoots that she turned into artistic shoots so it wouldn't seem like she was only a game girl. As long as they paid. The shoots were typically in hotel rooms and, although many of the photographers were professional, others were shooting her for no more reason than to serve as their game before the game, so when the shoot was complete, they expected the game. Hannah always kept her canvas backpack close, so if need be she could adequately defend herself with the mace and a blade she also kept on hand. If they refused to pay her, then she started destroying the room until they gave in. Though modeling of this sort might seem like a dangerous line of work, it paid well, as well as or better than doing extras, even the game. The clients couldn't touch her, merely look, and they would do that anyway. Their scrutiny accumulated to make her, so why not? When she was on stage or having her photograph taken, Hannah felt in control. The men became naïf little boy puppy dogs.

Unwarrantable, overstimulated, and eager to please. But when she stepped off the stage or when the camera was lowered, the puppies turned back into ravenous men. She knew that they would say or do anything to play the game with her, and she moved from one to the next, giving each a hint of it. Revolving her wiles to tap out each benefactor and their often-groveling virility. What they didn't know is that she ached for the game too, needed it like a child seeking parental approval while playing, so the men were actually the ones in control. She kept moving from club to club so that the discarded regulars would not realize the descending premium of her own consuming desires. Hannah used a different stage name at each place, each stage name from a Velvet Underground song. Candy, Jane, and Stephanie, but she kept Louise and Caroline in reserve and rarely used them since *Squeeze* was only a pseudo-Velvets record. A few cops were recently trying to get her to dance for their private parties, promising a lot of money, but Hannah sweetly brushed them off with caution. She was worried that they wouldn't take the snub much longer and that she might not have a choice. The word among the other dancers was that there was actually little money involved, if at all, because NOPD expected freebies, there were large turn-outs at the private parties, and they'd all be expecting the game. One right after another.

I learned all of this and more (well, most of it, and the rest is solid speculation) before we arrived at the World's

Fair gates featuring mermaids and water gods at the foot of Canal Street. Hannah laid her burdens down, unmasked them, and did it like she had an aversion to emotion, then produced the two pricey season passes that she quickly explained away by claiming that a friend gave them to her. As opposed to the usual manner of this type of engagement, the longer the evening continued, the quieter and more elusive she became, rather than the other way around. It seemed that revealing the earthy truths about the game and how she made money didn't feel exposing whatsoever to her, but actually served in her mind as the quick establishing of a wall of distance to set us apart, to be blatantly provocative and make it clear that I was daytime, she was nighttime, and this was her predisposed narrative to convey it. Or maybe her interest in me brimmed early on. We rode the largest Ferris Wheel in the world, danced poorly to Clifton Chenier's bluesy zydeco at the Jazz tent, huddled in the cable car across the river (rather than my preference of taking the significantly lower to ground monorail around the fairground, which held no chance of being stranded above the Mississippi like the cable cars), walked around eating, and ended it all by marveling at the fireworks display. All of it a feast of wonder. She smoked the entire night like she'd never seen a lighter and could only light a fresh cigarette from the remaining stub. Not too long ago, I'd smoked, if it can legitimately be called that, but no longer. It was simply a two year long affectation that resulted in burning holes in half of my limited wardrobe. Hannah singed me more than any cigarette could, though, initially by the sad side of her matter-of-fact desirability (she must've read it on me, because she put me on notice, Don't be one of those guys that wants to rescue me), then as we watched the fireworks and stars while she squinted, having lost her glasses, and mused, I love *Beauty and the Beast*. You know, the old movie that looks like it was dipped in silver. The director Cocteau once said something like, *We see the constellations, but the stars that form the constellations don't know that they do.* It was too obvious a reply, but I couldn't resist, Do you think any two given people can automatically form part of a larger shape? It depends, but I'll bet two people marked with the same sign, two Scorpios, form two claws, of course, but the third Scorpio's the stinger. Anyway, does it matter? Lips lie. Men only want one thing.

I knew that with her sublime mistrust she considered me another transparent little boy puppy dog, no more than a benign viper, but that made me want her more, with her constant red glow, her face like Eve's face. I would've said or done anything at that point to play the game with her (and still would), but she was several moves ahead, unexpectedly asking me to drop her off a couple streets from the block where I found her at so that she could stretch her legs, then quickly jumping out of the car and politely thanking me for a nice time, turning to the sidewalk before I could respond in any fashion other than driving on home with a meandering smile and a gentleman's ache, an affliction of longing. I suppose that I'm only the most recent of a discarded populace to have been left in her wake, but one evening with her only built up my appetite for another.

DAY 13

The one aspect of driving a cab that's proven the most difficult for me is also the chief expectation of the customer, getting from the pick-up spot to the destination directly and quickly. I understand without question why the passenger desires this structure, but the approach seems a limiting notion and it bores. No more than a token contribution at guiding each of them beyond the surface of the city to the reach beneath the streets. I'm neither terse nor efficient in the way I think or speak, so why would I pursue a quick common route from say a bar on Frenchmen Street to a hotel on Canal Street, when instead we can have the pleasure of seeing the collapsed balcony spilling off of the house over at Barracks and Burgundy Streets, the gaslight glow in select blocks, or follow a pattern antithetical to the guiding expectation of the streets' layout? Different ways to recover knowledge. This isn't a tactic to pad the fare and, in fact, all but the drunkest of passengers or those peculiarly intimidated by the Quarter's layout (ill-perceiving the grid-like old town of limited building scale as an inscrutable metropolis and its one-way streets as competing solutions to a multi-directional maze), all but these inept customers question me eventually, some suspicious and others quizzically surprised. I'm usually too impressed to take offense when they question the route or actually recognize a landmark or business that we've already passed once. Don't mistakenly think that I'm trying to be any sort of tour guide. That would be too exact a routine, well mostly, except for the guides that shift their stories to random buildings, relocating history and lore to less congested blocks to avoid the other tour groups and potential wait. My driving style is contrary to that of those cabbies who don't actually know the streets, because I'm well aware of the best to-and-from courses, which are mostly throughout the same blocks anyway. Instead, with or without fares, I like to pass the time by spelling my name with the car's route or driving a pattern, maybe a nice stair-step, on one end of the Quarter, and then its mirror image on the other end, creating new ways to view, interpret, and address the city, though I would never reveal this. Imagine the response to my reply of, Yes, we're back where we started from and moving parallel to Barracks, the street we turned off of, but in an opposite direction, river bound. Don't be alarmed. Next I'll loop back up on Esplanade, and then make a left on Dauphine. I assume you realize how a capital A is formed. I'm not driving like an ox intentionally. If it comes to the point of potentially losing the fare, then turning off the meter and spouting off a silly insider tidbit tale (wait until you hear about the scandal that happened at this house) massages their declarative and to-the-point perceptions of my navigation. I can understand being uninterested in matters of chance or the cracking open of different ports of entry, but you'd think that a few more customers might not mind a most unconventional way to rise above the conventional and applaud my unfortunate originality at being arch with limited knowledge.

DAY 14

I carried the awkward weight of a schoolboy's crush on Eve for years, but the summer before my sophomore year when she was but a semester from graduating high school, the crush became an awakening. There's no way for delicacy of disclosure other than to say that peculiar honesty is its own virtue. After I finished a five mile training run one afternoon, Eve called out from her porch, beckoning with the promise of frozen grapes. There was little time before my band practice, but I wanted to relax for a bit and catch up. We met in her grassy front yard under a ginkgo tree, and years later I haven't stopped musing fondly about hearing of Jorge Luis Borges for the first time, as well as why the short stories of Melville and Bruno Schulz mattered, the literary talk coupled with the considerably more banal (but leaving no less of a striking recall) instant headaches from eating the frozen fruit too quickly.

The sharpest element of this indelicate memory which is more than a memory, sharp enough to hold as much indelible and formative sway as reading the works of Borges eventually would, is that of Eve rising and returning to her house for more grapes. When she was midway there, she walked into a brilliant sunglare, surrounding her with a saint-like aura for a ferocious instant, the saturation of light causing her black dress to become momentarily sheer. My eyes dropped and heart widened, seeing her lower curves ever-so-briefly but clearly, my first view of any part of the female form normally covered. Granted this was no more than a kernel, but undisputedly an unexpected coronation of flesh, a new consciousness literally unveiled. I became immediately interested in the occasional infatuations provided by chance pleasures of this type or the lurid fevered ruminations of such, organizing a mental space to make my way through these boundless thoughts. Sex as an uppercase word held little sense previously (I looked askance at the crude bragging tales certain boys told at school) and it would confound for years, but I knew this had something to do with it and this I could handle. So began my entry into the universal vice, a marvelous craving of the fairer sex unadorned by clothing, craving that would occasionally dissolve my common sense. This in itself wasn't unique, but it's a safe assumption that most of the less-fairer sex (who like me, revisited these thoughts privately and reconciled them with desperate Onanistic reveling in the pleasure realm) weren't leering while also free-associating *naked, neighbor, native, nascent, natal, napalm.* My wholesome crush on Eve transformed to an unspoken pleading ache (quizzically noticed by its recipient but unreciprocated), eventually meeting its match in the stories of Borges, which came to provide a welcoming literary cold shower, as reading his philosophical prose, mostly stricken of carnality and laden with erudite concerns, served well to de-escalate my lustiness and sublimate transient concerns toward the contemplative.

On that summer day of awakening, Eve was only three months away from another heart surgery. While she was under the knife, I read the Bruno Schulz stories from her lent hardcover to feel connected, though I didn't understand them then. I read them to her in the hospital also, unaware that the dust jacket's cover art was a mere glimpse of the usual obsession portrayed in Schulz's artwork. Were Eve to have shown me a monograph of the Schulz-faced inadequate men with their furtive yearnings and servant-like subjugation to unattainable women, I'd likely have been shocked at a telling book of mirrors, by the idea that the bounteous vine of desire led others around by their noses too, and also left them with writhing consternation beyond frozen headaches.

Although it was expected, around six years later, when her heart gave out too soon at age 22, it wasn't desire I felt, but a triggered retching, an immense void, and a primal need to flee, to escape from Indiana. I couldn't handle attending the funeral and seeing Eve buried, but showed up early to offer private eulogy to her in the casket and also gawk at the new rectangular hole dug in the cemetery down the street, hours before the mourners arrived to grieve and shiver. Her parents asked me to be a pallbearer, and I'd weakly consented, but at the time she would've been lowered into the winter ground, I was racing due West, away.

DAY 15

Everyone here has a least one story of a previous life, most people several. Don't trust anyone without multiple histories or those who are responsibly certain. New Orleans is one of a few cities which attracts those with versatile lives, an expected stop along the way for at least a little while. It's a place where opposites of one's nature meet, organically resolve their contradictions, and find a way to coexist, if not bind. Not for everyone, certainly. Though many come here for a coveted reconciliation of this type, others do so expressly to avoid it.

My how-I-got-here tale is fairly simple compared to most, but also more harrowing. I decided it was time to get away from Indiana and see the country along the way, so I loaded up my few belongings and drove to San Francisco. A teaching job had been quickly lined up. My parents weren't to be counted on, and I wasn't so free and easy to play at relocating to a new city without certain advance stability. After bouncing from one flophouse to another, getting more and more fed up with the stumbling racket, I decided to buy a houseboat. A simple one. Nothing fancy. I didn't consider the problems that might come from living in the marina, particularly an upset stomach, but it was certainly unexpected for the Lady Howard to take on water in the middle of the night three days after I bought her. I can't actually swim, more of a flail and kick routine of minor forward motion, but that was enough to bridge the close distance to the dock. I owned few possessions before, but they immediately limited to only my car and the dripping sweats worn to bed. The Coast Guard looked into the cause of the sinking vessel and discovered a sizable hole with a temporary patch job that held long enough to sell the houseboat to a dupe willing to pay cash. No one in law enforcement was interested in pursuing the seller, but in spite of myself I had an obsessed sense of justice that few beyond a young person hold. It took a couple months of walking and talking, picking up stray tips, and connecting loose ends, before persistence paid off, and I eventually found the guilty party up in Sausalito. I was a hit of the Bay Area for a few weeks then and didn't have to pay for my drinks, what with the *Chronicle* doing a serialized spread on the manhunt, complete with my picture included. Since the newspaper mentioned the interview's location (Specs' bar in North Beach), a stream of p.i.'s tried to hire me. It was like a Humphrey Bogart movie, but without the masculine charm and femme fatales. There were so many rumpled suits shuffling into the bar for me that I toyed with the idea of coasting on the publicity and opening my own detective firm until I remembered my usually-yielding manner. It was nice to be in the limelight initially, but it soon felt unworthy being known on the streets, fitting in, unable to exist as an anonymous recluse, plus the regulars at Specs were getting fed up with the nonsense, so I declined it all and made arrangements, secured a position almost 2,000 miles away in New Orleans, and left without a word to anyone.

I know I appear to be good-natured, but it's only because I'm out in public the limited times that I feel good-natured. It's what I do. People encroach. I'm unsociable. I resign their company or that particular existence and return to my natural habitat. Swept away by the great indoors. Drunk on the still air in my mouth. At the moment, juggling my mind and scratching silly trifles in this notebook to save my head.

DAY 16

Melville's *The Confidence Man* is the story of a group of con men aboard a steamboat sailing down the Mississippi River, the sinuous almost-tail of which ribbons alongside New Orleans. If the seasoned crocodile-smile tricksters would've reached the city, they'd have more than met their match, for our grifters are second to none, regardless of color of collar. William Faulkner, whose presence looms larger and longer than his brief residency in this northernmost Caribbean outpost, wrote one novel of the child-like city by virtue of its residents. *Mosquitoes* is considered by no one to be one of Faulkner's better works, but it serves as another fine example of isolate-your-characters-on-water-and-see-what-happens.

What's next to be written after this day in December 1984? A continent or peninsula cracks loose and floats out into the ocean before exiling itself to a land mass, a houseboat's built on the backs of a trained crocodile team, or a ship never returns to port, only to drift? These three possibilities in glowing combination feel aptly similar to the isolated voyage of steamy surrealism that is New Orleans life. In reality, we wouldn't have very far to float before arriving somewhere near, say Cabrera Infante's Cuba. It doesn't take much hunting to discover that 1) There were New Orleans colonists from Havana, 2) A few decades later one realization of the Saint-Domingue slave revolt was a doubling of New Orleans, in part from Haitian Cubans, and 3) Rumor has it that Cuban rum-runners were in high demand here during Prohibition (which never quite took hold in this city that drinks freely), slipping in via the same eastern swamps that the Spanish boats asserted themselves through a couple centuries past. It also bears mentioning that the bounce in Jelly Roll Morton's piano style, what he called the Spanish Tinge, came from the influence of Caribbean musicians, though to barely brush the surface of a fertile topic is criminal.

New Orleans is a puzzling canvas. It's geographically, culturally, and psychologically ringed off from country. Havana suits as well as any other proposed spiritual counterpart, so much so that, interestingly enough, New Orleans has the feel of an island which floated loose of its Caribbean constellation and ended up fusing itself to a foreign body, resulting in a misshapen form (like a man with a book for a head or a cat with a single fin upon its back), but more than a backwater curiosity piece to be kindly tolerated or actively despised by its new host. In actuality New Orleans' general resistance to prevailing trends and tones places the city in a unique position. Few have any confidence in New Orleans, neither in its geographical form nor people (we take exasperating comfort in those of blank charm who pensively resent or boldly condemn us), but it's an oracular city, so far behind the present day that everyone else keeps sailing along, catching, and sizing us up from time to time. Jelly Roll's defiant eye is always there, looking for a wandering fortune, faithful to the descent like the rest of us, singular in his accomplishments, though dual in his follies, typifying our scarred principles and alluring cures. Despite being well-defined, for better or worse, New Orleans seems to exist as a blank slate for outsiders to grasp and cast their own aspirations, pretences, and prejudices upon. A few of the outsiders always end up lingering, holding fast, and adding to the city's layers, despite the fact that New Orleans changes them more than otherwise, ingrains itself in them if for no more than confounding sustenance.

Though not every sentence needs to contain the ocean, we're going to continue to float along, since clarifying the mention of a certain reptile is overdue. *Cuba, crocodile, constellations, confidence man. Crocodile tears, crocodile lies, crocodile smiles. Also, crocodile mystique.* Our latitude might be directly in line with Cairo, Egypt, but alligators are the usual animals found in this region rather than crocodiles, and there's no record of Southerners ever deifying this particular lizard. If one interchanged *croc* for *gator,* as in, They caught another croc in Audubon Park, sunning itself by the fountain, it'd be incorrect and like expressing that New Orleans barbecue shrimp should taste like it was prepared with a tomato or vinegar-based sauce, or saying *trolley* instead of *streetcar.* It's pariah talk. The usual misparlance from drink sloshing stumblers, but a terrible faux pas if spoken by a new local.

At the same time, use of the crocodile as a symbol is far more prevalent and expected, whether metaphorically straightforward as in Felisberto Hernandez's short story about a pianist whose crying jags spawn a nickname, or more mysteriously so in the works of De Quincey and Bruno Schulz. The crocodile is also employed as a metaphor of deception, indicating seeming trustworthiness, yet actually containing ulterior motives, cloaked as a man of the people until the opportune moment arrives and the liberator is revealed as false. This is the case in the 18th century apocalyptic allegory *Le Crocodile*, depicting The Crocodile as representing the low material world vanquished by upright mystics. Before The Crocodile is finally defeated by the adepts, author Louis Claude de Saint-Martin introduces fantastical elements like a plague of books which turns all the tomes of Paris into paste that is eaten by the city's residents, bringing about mass Babelspeak. Also, a number of the virtuous are swallowed by The Crocodile, and they travel through the limitless creature as if through purgatory.

The crocodile is likewise portrayed, though less fantastically, with expatriate Cabrera Infante's essay *Bites from a Bearded Crocodile* referenced in The Interview, in which the author, a former adherent of the Revolution, scathingly takes Castro to task for bringing about the decline of a literary renaissance as part of turning into an authoritarian regime, with the typical accoutrements like show trials and censorship boards. The Castro government held particular animus for homosexuals, especially artists. A police unit under the name Social Scum Squad unleashed the Night of the Three P's, a round-up of arresting all those considered pimp, prostitute, or pederast, many of whom ended up in concentration camps and worked sugarcane plantations. Anyone with the means or method fled Cuba. Others such as poet Heberto Padilla were assisted by U.S. intervention requests on their behalf to allow for a front door exit, so to speak.

When reading this essay prompted from The Interview, I was struck by one line spoken by Castro to Padilla when the two met on the verge of the dictator permitting the writer to leave the country. Referring to Padilla's house, Castro said, *Neither a book nor a brick will be touched*. His intent may have been literal, but I can't help but think that the bearded crocodile was speaking in an unintentionally associative manner. The common Freudian slip. *Books, bricks, beard, buried*. If one considers books as bricks in a threatening way, is there any difference ultimately between censoring and disallowing access to literature as compared to deftly devaluing and distracting from it, and do these two routes simply illustrate degrees of authoritarianism or multiple means to a single end? Am I unknowingly wandering inside The Crocodile? Are we all?

DAY 17

Hannah said, I'm the only child of a white Cancer father and a black Leo mother, and neither astrologically racial group seemed to fit, so I felt perpetually at odds and without need of sadness to stay sad. The disharmony of being named in a way that endeared Hannah to neither group stretched the tightrope further. Hannah was adamant that she would get out of the West End and also away from Louisville, a plain place, as soon as she was old enough. When she was all of seven years old, her parents separated due to her father's violent tendencies, and though Hannah wasn't supposed to see him, she moved in with her father by the age of thirteen. Her mother was terribly hurt, although Hannah explained that she wanted to be out of that part of the city, and her father's apartment downtown in Old Louisville wasn't far away. The depositing of a child into one particular womb, much less locale, is no more than a gamble in which the child is at the mercy of odds, and Hannah knew that her dice roll came up short. Louisville, especially the West End (the half of the city in decline after being virtually abandoned by businesses and any of the populace that could afford to move east after the devastating flood back in 1937), didn't look like her, talk like her, or feel like her. This was in a general sense, but it was the group she privately dubbed the psychohicks that particularly caused her to feel consternation and wanderlust. They were rough dangerous characters, most of whom came from the country or Appalachian region to the city for jobs or action. Hannah found it ironic that the rural areas were considered pastoral and holy, because so many of those she knew who hailed from that terrain were walking time bombs. Due to her mother's vacuum cleaner sales conferences, typically held in places like the Bahamas or New Orleans, Hannah grasped for the occasional view outside by accompanying her mother whenever possible, once old enough to explore on her own. Hannah wears her hair in one long pigtail on occasion because of seeing an Asian woman doing the same on a beach in the islands and was told by a fortune teller that she, Hannah, was Oriental in another life. New Orleans was the first city in which she felt that people were like her, they were shades like her, and they spoke their minds like her. After returning home from these trips, the wrecking concerns returned and Hannah's anger brimmed, so she joined an after-school boxing program at the neighborhood gym as a release. She maintained no relationships during high school, save for the occasional long distance one, so the gym and a way out became her mutual obsessions while she was a patient of impatience until graduation.

Before ending up in Southern Louisiana, Hannah lived in Las Vegas. Despite knowing rough neighborhoods in that Gemini city, she was taken aback by the area her as-is New Orleans apartment (no appliances, rotting floorboards, flickering electricity) was situated in, considering that it was filled with unaccountable characters (the New Orleans version of Havana's so-called social scum), yet on a key street in the supposed showcase of the city. The hotel operators, pre-existing and newcomers, expected a boom from the stream of World's Fair attendees, so they'd been buying up cheap rundown buildings, evicting the tenants, and making minor cosmetic upgrades to give the appearance of justification for higher short-term rates. Many landlords were doing the same. A seedy and violent stretch of North Peters Street (up until a year back, so dangerous and rundown that rent for Hannah's entire third floor loft was a pay-only-in-cash pittance), was transformed the week Hannah was out of town for a photo shoot in Los Angeles. She returned to find relative quiet, no mayhem, and the entrance's iron gate wrapped in a chain and padlocked. The word on the street was that, as the river stretch of derelict metal wharf buildings, sturdy brick warehouses, and everything otherwise, were being torn down or arsoned to prepare for the fair, the street creatures were gradually shifted to the block in which Hannah lived. This had been happening prior to her moving in and was why the influx of low-level pimps, dealers, hookers, hustlers, thieves, junkies, and the like saturated and flourished, they'd been pushed out of other areas and heard that the 200 block of North

Peters was the anything goes zone. It was very much that for the year she lived there, the chaos building up for what in actuality was no more than a ploy by the feds for a surprise large-scale bust with buses, a New Orleans Night of the Three P's that luckily happened when Hannah was away. In spite of all of the near-river cleansing, fair attendance was low and housing costs avaricious, so rentals and hotels in the Quarter topped out at barely above half-occupied. Even with the ground shift of these changes and seeing the Quarter transformed into a modern cordiality machine to attract tourists, Hannah and I enjoyed a wonderful time at the fair, surrounded mostly by locals.

Before she clammed up, Hannah said, My first New Orleans apartment and the whole as-is system of real estate seems indicative of the city at large. You can pay pennies for a neglected room, feel like you're in the center of the universe, but at some point it'll disappear along with everything you own, only you don't know when. All you can do is live in the moment and hope for a little joy before the padlock clicks in place. In any case, there's always another room. In this city nothing ever changes. At least that used to be the case, before the smell of money came around.

I thought that I saw a flicker of Hannah's soul a few times that night, but I may have been confused. My power and mystery, limited as it is, comes from unrevealing, refraining from speaking to cover myself up (although I opened up to her that night), but Hannah verbalises to do the same. I suspect that she reinvents herself with every conversation, creates a lark of truth to prevent the appearance of a doleful life, but I'm dogged by the bald possibility that rather than having an eye for deception, Hannah is an enigma of honesty, peddling an immense innate doctrine of consistency renounced, caprice embraced, and facts disposable, this coexisting alongside a refreshingly incautious utopian philosophy of genuine openness and candor personified. Each a perceptible reflection of the other. It's easier to believe that and keep distance from the mocking pain of knowledge, conceding that in her pale squinting eyes, I'm ferociously commonplace, a charitable toleration, worthy only of polite neglect.

DAY 18

My dreams have fallen into a rotation rhythm lately. The situation unspools in its usual fashion, then there are the Eve/Hannah dreams of both erotic desire and sun-drenched wistfulness (occasionally, a single head contains both of their faces, like the god Janus, similar though separate), but the most recent entry in the array involves an unfamiliar writer in a room. I've yet to decipher whether or not he's chosen isolation of his own accord or is being held captive, but his existence is limited to a small one-room structure of metal, defined only by its interior. His name is Mutter. He's not written this name, in fact he writes another, but Mutter emanates from him nonetheless with resonance and constancy. His room is doorless and contains only a desk with notepad and pen, small library, and a speaker/microphone device mounted to the wall opposite his desk. At any point he's asked questions about his writing and thoughts, always questions, by a dispassionate computerized voice of low quality, a cracked digital interrogation to which he's obliged to stand and answer. The savvy Mutter intelligently and meticulously responding is juxtaposed against his artificial inquisitor. There are never follow-up questions to his replies, merely different questions, and when there are no more questions, there is silence. The silence accompanies Mutter when he thinks, writes, or occasionally looks out the single window with satisfaction at the single tree, the tree always accompanied by darkness. His room, by comparison, is always brightly lit, and although he appears healthy, rested, and generally fit, it's unclear how he eats, sleeps, cleans, or removes his body's waste. This doesn't seem to bother him, and his general tone of character is one of acceptance and duty, of settling into noble years after seasons of being warmed by several suns. I wonder if his mind has replaced his digestive tract and intestines or if the letters he forms carry out these integral duties for him?

This is the sole dream that I don't understand presently. The others are perfectly clear. What is his puzzle? Am I Mutter or the voice, the tree or the window? Perhaps I'm none of these and this dream is a parable about being caught between, the endless loop of routine and literary dedication securing one to an endless present between two names, the negotiation of secret twins, as if both designations, past and future, cling to the shared head orbited by the loop. Now then, there's the matter of what it is that Mutter actually commits to paper day after day, beyond the name which isn't Mutter penned at the top of each page. The chief characteristic of his writing is its navigation with considerable musicality (pearls which are mostly elegant acquaintances but also hostile snarlers), to speak a language of migration, the wide talk of a winedark crawl. Canny transactions with the familiar silence of a tiny room.

Although this dream is of me (meaning it's mine, surfacing and receding through my own layers of consciousness), the writer Mutter's story is of him, so I'll reveal no more other than to say that the seeming best way to satisfactorily portray both his writing and answers to the voice is to characterize it all as the letter by letter unburying of a name.

DAY 19

C, t, b, d, r. C. Cuba, crocodile, constellations, confidence man. T. Tarot, 22, two-faced, taboo, The Pelican, the place. B. Books, bricks, beard, buried. D. Death, dirt. R. Rub.

They were pointing and waving at me like a scattered Greek chorus accusing, He's Guilty! I realized that in my panic and haste to remove the body from the house, grimace it into the trunk, and race off, I didn't remember to remove the cab magnets, so locals along the way were hoping for a lift. It was the 4th of November. *Fancy Nest, Follicle Need, Flighty Neighbor, Faust Necro, Film Noir, Fickle Name, Furious Noise.* My heartbeat a tympani roll, insistent and crescendoing to the crack of dual gunshots that continued cracking in my mind well after their initial blasts.

The first was the one that sprung me out of the car to jump the stoop steps and fling myself inside the unlocked house on Dauphine Street. When The Pelican initially went to the door with winking intent and was met by Hannah, she sunk noticeably but recovered and invited him in with a tender rub to the left of his jaw. After ten minutes or so came the single shot of gunfire. I followed his voice through the sparse careless parlor, down the short hallway, into the kitchen, and found her lying on the floor and bleeding from her right arm, a paring knife at her side, while he was crouched with his back to me, edgy and pleading repeatedly, Why'd you make me do it? She spoke through her teeth, clamping down on the pain, explaining desperately that she was leaving New Orleans, going to Havana, and her boyfriend was going with her. Taking this in, I was anything but emboldened by impunity. Shoot a shooter, me? It's not my way. What would I shoot or attack him with? Instead I began to shake, and then, as if magnified by mirrors, my shake shook. *C, t, b, d, r.*

Unsurprisingly, The Pelican sensed my presence and spun, training his gun on me and glowering, Get the fuck outta here. Back in the fucking car. Now! Hannah surprised both of us when she pointed at me and said, He's my boyfriend. We're moving to Havana. The Pelican's face of aggression and mine of fright merged to a single bewildered countenance. I was speechless, having become an instant beard for Hannah while he held me in his direct line of fire. He smirked and lowered his gun, stared at her woodenly, then down at the gun. She teared up, telling him she loved him, didn't know what she'd been thinking, and the two of them should go to Cuba. This broke his trance and the seething returned. He snatched the knife with his left hand and roughly slashed her right cheek, hissing, You two-faced tramp. You're not gonna ruin any more men. Go to your car and bring me the fucking registration, okay, boyfriend.

His request was perplexing, but I followed directions and then became further confused when he carefully folded my auto registration down to thumbnail size, bound it in tin foil, swallowed it, and washed it down with water, grinning after the last gulp. As her crying heaved and I remained in hands-up paralysis, he (a man who seemed most dangerous when he was deliberate) returned to his former position, leaned over and firmly grabbed her right hand, squeezed it around the gun's trigger and held it in place, with the barrel facing her. She called out when he yanked her arm up and spun the gun to jam it firmly against his forehead. With a demeanor as light and calm as I had witnessed from him, his last words were, Now look who's fucked. You've got nothing but crocodile tears, crocodile lies. You're gonna rub me out. I'm gonna make you do it. The gun connects you. The registration connects him. Three can't keep a secret when only one's dead. Especially when the dead man still talks. It's time for me to sleep, get my rest. Call the burial, dirt rest.

After a few frozen moments, I stumbled over and pulled his limp body off of her as she burst with horrified staccato gasping, crying, and screaming, the shot and her immediate accompanying start continuing to replay in my mind along with *C, t, b, d, r.* When she finally sat up, composed herself and spoke, she struck as being miles beyond my still-dazed speechless shaky state. You've got to get rid of the body. Not the river. Bury him. In the swamps. I'll take care of the gun. Then we'll be together. She looked at me through faded green eyes, hoping I'd comply, would do anything to be close to her and not contend that her words should be taken at other than face value. When the firmness of realization came to her, as of course it did, I sat beside her compliantly, guilelessly moved my head to her beckoning crimson right hand which caressed the underside of my chin, caressed it like she meant it, and I bent to her touch, warming to it too easily, like I always do no matter who, while she softly purred, I'll always remember the 4th of November. Now, go bury him and pack. Make sure to weight him down. When you get back, we'll head off to Havana together. Do you have a shovel at home?

I returned a couple hours later with a change of clothes, my dufflebag, and box of Vachal ex-libris in the back seat. Oh Eve, I've reached you again at last. I'm home. I was sweaty and exhausted but with adrenaline pushing, and then stunned to find the front door wide open, all the lights on, and her apartment a tossed overtaken mess, as if she'd made quick take-it-or-leave-it decisions. I assumed she'd be waiting for me after I finished, but no Hannah, and the kitchen looked like a charnel house. The November soil (off of Chef Menteur Highway, where you must have found the body by now if you've read this far) at the place was soft, so it'd presented no difficulties, but the physical action itself as well as its ramifications kept me pumped and jittery, though it felt like I was dishonoring the moonlight. I want to make it clear that before rolling him into the hole, I collected all of the 20 dollar bill halves since it was my money, but I did return the surprising letter also tucked in his pocket, one from the animal shelter thanking him for his donation. I expected that Hannah would be in a hurry but was surprised she wasn't at the little house on Dauphine Street, after what she'd said and all of the sufficient trouble I'd taken, surprised but with a sense of denial about what looked to be the case. No Hannah, but she'd be back soon. I slept there that night, tried to sleep I should say, on her couch in the parlor, so I didn't have to see the kitchen again, waking hourly with the expectation that she'd return soon. But she didn't return, so after a sinking morning, sunken afternoon, and an evening of waiting with hope growing ragged, I checked at the club she danced at and was told she hadn't been seen for days.

I'll admit to expecting her to show up, and every night I've been looping the block, clinging to the honest intentions of her hypothetical heart. Maybe there was a misunderstanding. But it's finally sinking into my fallow mind that this is what she does. She bounces. She's a cunning operator who bounces around and then never has to prove her dear hasty deceits. She's only in communion with betrayal. Or was she just scared? I thought that by proving myself to her with this deed, I was finally lucidly seizing the future with a piercing focus, boldly asserting control, a man of action, but instead I was executing confusion. I'm still confused. She's a wandering spirit, out there forming new constellations in a wider sky then I'll ever know. Did she go to Havana? I thought she was my port, but instead I'm the ship that drifts aimlessly in disenchantment to the tides of another. I'm always the cover, the beard, the idle pastime, the one they move on from.

This incident might be instructive at a future point were I not likely to repeat the identical course of action and expectation, again thinking it was a courage-headed step. The weak don't make avowals, though, but quietly follow those set by the strong. That isn't so much a maxim as it's an expected acknowledgment that some are born to act and others to respond, all spinning through well-traveled labyrinths, with confidence only in the known course.

DAY 20

I know how poorly I'd handle a court hearing, walking up the steps of the imposing building at Tulane and Broad Streets, anxiety rising, mired in the hallway, wondering if the judge bothered to show up that day, much less on time, anxiety rising, entering the indifferent courtroom after an indeterminate wait, anxiety rising, becoming increasingly stirred up knowing what comes next, anxiety rising enough that I'd probably tremulously collapse from the stress of it all. Granted, this scenario makes the improbable assumption that I'd actually make bail or avoid expected street justice meted out by The Pelican's fellow officers. If the unwieldy hurdle of the latter was surprisingly cleared (which is partly what the notebook is for), but not the former, I'd spend a year or so in the odious madhouse called Orleans Parish Prison, at the mercy of sadistic guards and coarse prisoners. I'd lose my apartment, eventually my car, and be broken by the time the case came to court. A weakened rather than hardened man. At that point, fainting would be strenuous beyond my capabilities. There's likely a prison guard version of The Pelican, assuming they care about anonymity there, and I'd be a probable recipient. I feel light-headed and guilty, a hair-shirt of the mind, with only simple examination of these possibilities. The only thing chiseled about me is my elephantine anxiety.

It does allow better understanding of Raskolnikov in *Crime and Punishment*, I mean the psychology of it all, of looming discovery, trying to sleep when anxiety's rising. To take a broad view, it then stands to reason that one's own actions ought to be mostly compatible with corresponding temperament, and it could be a tragic mistake to assert otherwise, extending beyond comforting torments, forcing disunity of nature. Use your space, but know your place. This sounds jarringly obvious on the face of it, but the contrary occurs all the time, whatever the reason that such ill-inspired behavior foolishly asserts itself to deny nature, like miscasting oneself in a role. Is there anything worse than an inflamed dreamer? The stars glitter as they should when the meek remain meek and the incorrigible, incorrigible. A combination of Dostoevsky, Karl Marx, and Robert Burton. Behavior by each, according to one's humors. The Anatomy of the Distribution of Temperaments. More commonly said, If you can't do the time, don't do the crime (there's no need to take the time to mine the well-trodden related ideas of only having the right if you have the might, or if this kind of villainous behavior can lead to liberation). It's an unjust truth, but anything otherwise is an incompatible extravagance. Although criminals can be civilians, civilians shouldn't be criminals. We civilians are neither inured nor savvy enough to deal with the institutionalized system, and this nature isn't easily camouflaged. For most of us, a required trip to the DMV or City Hall is sufficient, we're unequipped to handle the matter-of-fact wait-to-take-a-number-to-take-a-number bureaucracy if coupled with incarceration, much less the threat of the possibility of it, and though I'm not guilty, here I sit.

I can picture my mother tearfully exclaiming to my father across the kitchen table, I thought he was misdirected, but I had no idea he was capable of this? I can picture it strongly, both of them wearing a fresh crust of shame, that at this very moment, I'm internally responding to the image, pleading, You don't understand, mother. I'm not capable of the act. If I was calibrated that way, I'd be placid and abstract. I'm certainly not capable of serving hard time, but what I'm least capable of is this unconsummated relationship, the not-knowing, the outsized head games of living in anticipation, not-knowing whether or not this in between is the only country I belong to from now on. I'm actually not enigmatic, just sinking. I'm the Raskolnikov who didn't swing an axe, but will be considered the perpetrator regardless, that is if they find the sub rosa place, mother. But even if they don't, there's no consolation, no pleasingly visible end, what with all of the accompanying inner turmoil the possibility of discovery brings. It's the closest thing to purgatory on earth that I can imagine, a distressing morass of foreboding. I'm a master of maintaining unflappable theories, mother, but in real life I've remained as I am, wavering and incapable. There was overreaching, yes, but I was only a sucker for a face. I saw Eve again.

DAY 21

I'm not naturally drawn to cemeteries, despite the plentiful above-ground variety in New Orleans. Ornate headstones, much less gravestone rubbings don't hold appeal. Funerals especially repel me. So, I must come to terms with why the place, a crude burial spot, appeals. Why am I drawn to go back to the place and dig up the body, potentially attracting troublesome attention? Since you aren't me, you might think it no more than an obsessive compulsion to confirm that he remains there, not resting but decomposing without dignity. You might also speculate that I hold a deep need to get caught, so returning to the place would be for the chief reason of an alert to my complicity. There may be faint strands of both those assumptions at work, but one can only admit to what one knows.

I know I'm drawn to dig up and rebury the body, at least in part, to reexperience the initially-unexpected euphoria of the taboo. I know that the physical exertion, the power over another human, the expected approval from a woman I desired (and still do), for at least these reasons, I reached combustion, became drunk on the action, and crave that fiery cup again. I know that the rationale for this notebook is partly an excuse to return to the place, an act of necessity providing justifiable cover for a weakening into craven impulse. I know if I give in to a follow-up visit after the second trip to bury the errata notebook, then it'll become occasional habit, which will become repetition, which will become routine. I know I'm of weak stock and therefore must restrict myself in the same way of the other, older, restriction. I know I knew this around a decade ago, that although gravestone rubbings don't personally appeal, human rubbings do, with my role both that of paper and pencil. I know I avoid crowds, force myself to walk unoccupied sidewalks or in the streets, never take buses, stay away from Mardi Gras parades, and generally hermit myself from what I like, which is what I am. In New Orleans, anything goes, until it doesn't. This is a difficult city for innocent excursions anyway, what with all of the con artists of desire lurking around, trying to hide in public. Since this notebook may never be seen, I can divulge what cold introspection has revealed. I've justified this ongoing compulsion with a convenient theory rather than admit to actual arousal, legitimizing it away as an art project of life, although one mostly resisted, an updating of Max Ernst's technique of using frottage to add texture to his works, my version no more than a dismissing of conventional forms of public interaction and replacing them with traces of sensual tactility, hoping for the spontaneity of a pleasing stranger who might reciprocate, all of this deconstructing society. But really, the rub turns me on. Don't let my excuses and jostling belie a booming self-disgust. I know this transmuting of expression, hopeful cry of communication, wouldn't be seen as that of a visionary mind but a diseased one, a frenzied goat perpetually rutting. I know certain tendencies are considered −ism and −mania aberrations although seeming to me like perfectly natural behavior, so I cloister. I keep from certain situations and cloister, which is how I also must handle the place and the inclinations it's provoked in me. I know.

There's little doubt, at least in my mind, that the writers Cabrera Infante, Melville, and Bruno Schulz, as well as the artist Vachal, would fully understand the indicting impulses and searing cravings that arise, the chance for ruination, knowing we're all linked to this common story by different thirsts, all patriots to a nation of taboos (Who isn't, other than those who are anomalies or in denial?), and they'd cumulatively advise that one can either feed or starve the craving when it arises, though it can also be used to seed artistic work. Is there any question that this defined group didn't infuse its own work with impolite stirrings, that one impetus for their creativity, in fact, was as a means of sublimation, to release the capped-up cravings? I feel one with the ones who once sat as I sit here now, with the police scanner's volume turned to a hushed intimate cadence. It seems perfectly clear that what is in me will come out from me in defined form, so I'm obliged to free it, harness it, and purposefully tame it in certain fashion, if not respectable, at

least presentable. Otherwise, I'll be one more Scorpio fallen
into ruin from my own stinger, if I've not done so already.

DAY 22

An unexpected change in behavior has come about over the 22 days I've written these pages, initially thinking I was spending quiet mornings in cliché, weakly languishing in torment, hoping for modified composure, trying to correct perceptions that potentially wouldn't exist if I hadn't made a mistake of desire and dabbling. Do you have confidence in me, in what you've read? I'll miss the errata notebook and can't imagine burying it, though I must and this needs to happen quickly. That's no urgency scam. The notebook has become me, though, another form of Raymond Russell, but from a different observational angle. The notebook is Raymond Errata and, though parting with it'll be like losing a limb, I hope to be able to read properly again, hope that a writing dabble hasn't ruined the sustained pleasure of a good book. Since starting this notebook, it's become distressingly impossible to read with focus. I become jabbed with thoughts of the notebook, then return back to the book page at hand, stopping often throughout to jot down an exceptional phrase, ruminating over an idea that might be adapted, and critiquing how a particular sentence might be better written. It appears that I can't be both reader and writer, which isn't the same as a writer who reads. One suffers for the other to flourish. Of this, there's no middle ground. Not only is it troubling for the sake of sabotaging escapism and slowing down my learning tremendously, but also because of alarmingly turning my own pages into a closer resemblance to literature than the intended mere telegramming of events (granted, telegramming seems to be the highest aspiration for the present day prevailing breed, that mouth of rotting teeth, it's a pity when writers don't value words, attempting little beyond a 4/4 time plunk, plunk, plunk, plunk in print, and more so when readers seek no more than those writers).

It's time to change out the books bricked into the support piers. The weather and bugs have left only wiggy pages amidst intact covers, but I don't have replacement titles ready to insert yet. None of this is to say that I consider myself any sort of emerging writer (that would be a flimsy unworthy title), to which the proper response would be sheer mirth. Who am I other than a lazy but committed scribbler, conveying a core specimen of first draft faith, but letting the letters labor to do the real work, the form-altering nature of things? Any lucky eloquence is due to the letters themselves. Who'd be interested in my dim insensible thoughts? I'll never be a writer or a cousin to mankind. No, I'm not confiding speciously (a lovely word for an ugly manner) when I say that I've no wish to be a writer. There's surely no market for pastiche-strewn pages. Leave the mortal arts to me. Let others perform the wound-picking struggle, claim alleged virtues, be confident in their weaknesses, and libel their friends and neighbors. Likewise, let the nocturnal habits of the alphabet speak with the tongue of the moon, transmuting and reversing my common speech, skipping beyond the heroic, back to the core to evolve forward, but let this happen after my part with it is done. Let the names be named in the dirt and may they never be uncovered.

What if the notebook might remain buried, never found, if I could merge with it and make Raymond unnecessary? The two of us as one. Never found. Raymond Errata, Errata Raymond, alloyed for language. Language that no longer communicates. This our mutual devotion. Would that it could be done, but I must bury the notebook, Raymond Errata. Its importance will have been served by doing so, both as a self-imposed drying-up of my counterfeit encounter with the pen and to bear the original purpose of an incrimination remedy. Yes, Raymond Errata must be buried. Though it's obvious that I'm of mixed mind about this, follow through is necessary. If my pilfered books can serve two purposes, aesthetic and pragmatic, as literature and as bricks, then why not bury this notebook as mutual tribute to text and a righting of the record? *C, t, b, d, r.*

But what does it mean to bury a book of this sort? And what does it also mean that solitude, insomnia, and a corpse as subjects by themselves, much less as an unbridled triumvirate, are considered well-worn? Despite being in my sunrise years, I'm quickly learning that clichés only exist until they first become personal, then possessive. My solitude, my insomnia, the dead body I buried (believe otherwise at the moment, but wait until your strength withers and you recant your confidence). There are no clichés of life, only in language, which is no more than lazy language, folksy homilies of sloganed familiarity. Life, on the other hand, surprises when an individual's gathered fragments gain the coherency of strength, and startles when its unpredictability permits or is unable to prevent the occasional chance clustering of those who lean toward common tribes, these endlessly rippling constellations linking naturally to the unnatural, and it's more so surprising when any two or more individual's imbalances allow for any sustained sharing of the echoing fabric of peace and madness, tragedy and triumph that presents itself, cleaving us like a written word, goaded, pillaged, and occasionally restored. Flux stars fall into the internal laws of syntax.

LAVENDER INK TITLES

COMING IN 2013

What Else Do You Want? by John Miller (with Fell Swoop)

Industrial Loop by Joel Dailey (with Fell Swoop)

Under The Sky Of No Complaint by Richard Martin (with Fell Swoop)

lavenderink.org

CPSIA information can be obtained at www.ICGtesting.com
Printed in the USA
LVOW062313051012

301754LV00003B/1/P